That DINOSAUR NT!

Buster Books

Edited by Frances Evans

Designed by Jack Clucas

Cover design by John Bigwood

With special thanks to Josephine Southon
and Derrian Bradder

For Isaac — LM

For Eleanor and Emily — RM

First published in Great Britain in 2021 by Buster Books,
an imprint of Michael O'Mara Books Limited, 9 Lion Yard,
Tremadoc Road, London SW4 7NQ

W www.mombooks.com/buster   F Buster Books   T @BusterBooks   @buster_books

Text copyright © Lily Murray 2021
Illustrations copyright © Richard Merritt 2021
Layout and design copyright © Buster Books 2021

A CIP catalogue record for this book is available from the British Library.

ISBN: 978-1-78055-749-6

1 3 5 7 9 10 8 6 4 2

This book was printed in July 2021 by Bell & Bain Limited, 303 Burnfield Road,
Thornliebank, Glasgow, G46 7UQ, United Kingdom.

That DINOSAUR HAS TALENT!

Written by Lily Murray

Illustrated by Richard Merritt

Eliza Jane was a lucky child.

She lived in a town that was **wonderfully** wild.

It had rivers and trees and parks to explore,
But best of all were the . . .

DINOSAURS!

There were pterosaur taxis, sweeping the skies ...

... Troodon teachers, clever and wise,

Ankylosaur builders, sauropod cranes,
Stegosaur buses, stomping down lanes,

Raptors in restaurants, dishing out cakes,
And plesiosaur boats, cruising the lakes.

Every dinosaur had a job to do,
All except Parry ... who was lonely and blue.

Eliza Jane noticed. She heard his sighs.

She saw his sorrow, the tears in his eyes.

"Oh, let me help you!" begged Eliza Jane.

"I think I know how, if you'll let me explain."

"I'll find you a job –
there's so many to choose!
You could paint the town
or shine people's shoes?

Work in a café
as one of the cooks,
Run the town library
handing out books?

Become a barber,
cutting fabulous styles,
Or train as a dentist,
making beautiful smiles?"

But no matter what Parry tried to master,

It always ended in **TOTAL**

DISASTER!

"Don't worry, Parry, there's a job for you.
We've all got talent when we **LOVE** what we do."

Parry turned his back. He stared at the floor.
He slumped his shoulders. He sniffed some more.
Eliza Jane hugged him. "Come home with me.
You can stay at mine and I'll make you tea."

She gave him hot milk and warm buttered bread.
Parry smiled wide as she tucked him in bed.

But Eliza Jane couldn't sleep that night,
Too busy thinking how to make things right.
Then all of a sudden, by the light of the moon,
She heard a beautiful, **toe-tapping** tune.

She opened her window and
there on the street,
Parry was **DANCING**
on feather-light feet.

His crest blew out music that rang through the air,
A wonderful song that he longed to share.

Eliza Jane thought, "I wonder why

he's kept this a secret? Is he just too shy?"

She could see that Parry was lit up — aglow!

"What this dinosaur needs is a **TALENT SHOW**."

All week, Eliza Jane plotted and planned.
She put up posters and hired a band.

She made Parry a costume, rainbow bright,
With sparkling sequins that shone in the light.

At last the day came for the **TALENT SHOW**.

Eliza Jane smiled, "Let's give it a go!"

Dinosaurs had come from all over town —
a juggling Jobaria, a T. rex clown,

A Gallimimus group
doing high kicks,
A Mapusaurus performing
magic tricks ...

... He disappeared in
a puff of blue smoke.
Next came a Troodon,
telling terrible jokes.

Finally, it was Parry's
turn to perform.
Eliza Jane whispered,
"You'll take them by storm!"

But Parry stood still, as if turned to stone.
Eliza Jane saw he couldn't do it alone.

She climbed on the stage, and stood by his side.
"You've got this," she said, her eyes full of pride.
"You don't need to worry about taking part.
Just close your eyes, and follow your heart."

Parry took a breath. He tapped his hooves.
Soon he was busting his very own moves!

He swirled and he twirled, he sang out his tune.
Everyone cheered! The judges all swooned.

Everyone clapped, hooting louder and louder.
Eliza Jane said, "I couldn't be prouder."

Now if you visit Eliza Jane's town,

Take a stegosaur bus, see a T. rex clown.

You can meet a Troodon, clever and wise,

Ride a pterosaur taxi up through the skies,

Try a raptor restaurant, taste their cakes,
Swim with plesiosaurs in sparkling lakes.
And then, of course, you really *must* go . . .

...TO PARRY'S
AMAZING DINOSAUR SHOW!

Parry's happy at last, but it's not down to fame.

It's because he's found **friendship**
with Eliza Jane.

Parasaurolophus
(pa-ra-saw-rol-off-us)

Parry is a young Parasaurolophus. It's thought that this dinosaur may
have been able to produce sounds from the crest on its head.

Ankylosaur
(an-kie-loh-sore)

Gallimimus
(gal-lee-meem-us)

Jobaria
(joh-bahr-ee-uh)

Mapusaurus
(mah-puh-sore-us)

Plesiosaur
(plee-see-oh-sore)

Pterosaur
(teh-roh-sore)

Raptor
(rap-tore)

Stegosaur
(steg-oh-sore)

Tyrannosaurus rex
(tie-ran-oh-sore-us rex)

Troodon
(troe-oh-don)